Grim Fairy Tales

Adam Nicke

Born on the Lupercalia – the Roman festival of the wolf – in 1967, Adam Nicke spent an unhappy and lonely childhood in a series of isolated houses along the Welsh Border. During this difficult period, he sought refuge in literature and within his imagination.

When he grew up, his artistic tendencies were first expressed in the designing and making of clothing, most notably for Wayne Hussey of The Mission. Later, he turned to writing fiction which explores an inner realm of moods and anxieties, and the feelings of guilt experienced by characters coming to terms with an alienating world. He has a degree in literary studies from the University of the West of England.

The illustrator, Jocelyn Almond (1956–2014) is probably best known for her illustrations in Vortex science fiction and fantasy magazine in the late 1970s. In the 1980s and 1990s her pictures and stories appeared in various small press publications and in art exhibitions both in Britain and in Europe. She also published books on the Tarot and on Egyptian paganism, and for over twenty years served as a Priestess in the Fellowship of Isis.

Grim Fairy Tales

by
Adam Nicke

with illustrations by
Jocelyn Almond

Adam Nicke Publishing

First published by Tyrannosaurus Rex Press
1995, this new edition published by
Adam Nicke Publishing 2017
adamnicke@gmail.com

Illustrations by Jocelyn Almond
Cover design by Adam Nicke

Imprint: Independently published

ISBN   978–1–54477–111–3   (paperback)

*Dedicated to both my mother and my
maternal grandmother, Susan and Pat,
both of whom I miss dearly but who
would have both shared my delight in
seeing this little book back in print.*

Acknowledgements

I would like to thank the Gothic Society for first putting me in print; David Hurst for taking the photograph of me in 1991 which appears on the back cover; and lastly, G. E. Vane and Jocelyn Almond of Tyrannosaurus Rex Press without whom none of this would have ever come to fruition.

Contents

The Jewellery Box

How dearly as a young man did I love this time of year! The autumn equinox, the golden month of September, when all the world seemed resigned to death; when all her young offspring kissed goodbye to a dear mother who had nurtured them so tenderly while they had lain on her soft maternal bosom, unaware that their mutual ageing would so soon destroy their innocence.

Even then, in those far distant days, I identified with such dignified decay. It was only later that the crimson hues and twilight golds would hang heavily on my heart and remind

---

me of a more tangible death. Even as I now write, some sixty years later, the memory of that golden era haunts me still, burning like a candle in the darkness; and I, like a moth, am forever drawn to the flame, its very glow all that sustains me, all that haunts me, binding me to it as surely as would any chains.

Then came my twenty-fifth year. Now a man, I found myself sanguine enough, if a little prone to bouts of melancholia; then, one hot summer's day, I met Ophelia, fluttering into my life as light and as airy as the most beautiful butterfly. I, having come from a good family with good prospects, was deemed a suitable beau by my future father-in-law. It was to our eternal happiness, for it quickly transpired that Ophelia loved me as I her. After a brief courtship, during which we spent many happy hours walking by the river, always chaperoned - Ophelia had her reputation to think of - we married. How my heart lightens still to think of that long hot summer, sun penetrating the lace of Ophelia's parasol, gently kissing the face I also longed to touch and kiss.

The following six months were the happiest of our lives. I never thought a mortal such as I worthy of so much pleasure.

The food I ate with Ophelia was ambrosia, the drink nectar, as long as my own Venus was there with me. But my happiness was yet incomplete until one frosty February morning when Ophelia told me that the fruit of our love would be born to us that autumn. Our joy seemed absolute.

All summer, Ophelia and I walked along those river banks, across those same summer meadows, those Elysian fields. Surely no god could ever have crafted such bliss! Every time I gazed at Ophelia my heart overflowed, like an overfilled ciborium. I would have died a thousand deaths for her.

Even now, these memories slice me in two, for a month before the birth, Ophelia fell ill. She became pale and ashen, seemingly overnight. Her once beautiful countenance became painful to observe. As much as I loved her, love this time was not enough: if Ophelia did not recover, the birth would kill her.

But it was not to be. There was nothing any doctor could do: Ophelia died giving birth to our child. The child drew a single breath and joined my dear Ophelia. The only woman I had ever loved was taken from me that autumn day. The trees wept tears of blood, as my tears ran crystalline.

And now all I have is Ophelia's jewellery box and beloved gemstones. How lovingly we bought them together, I to frame her idolised symmetry, she to please the man she loved.

Little did I then think that these pitiful rocks would become the single thread to bind me to my dead love. I love these stones now as I loved her, and as she loved them. Every day I press them to my heart, and caress them as once I did Ophelia.

The black onyx, this beautiful variety of chalcedony: the exquisite striations of the stone remind me of her perfectly manicured nails and the slender fingers that once tenderly touched my face. I press it to my eye and see only the happy times, the sylph, the naiad that I loved and married.

The tiger's eye reminds me of her long golden-brown tresses and of long, golden days. How I wish I had them still!

The carnelian, this translucent orange chalcedony: how those flames framed her face! Turner never painted such flames, nor Burne-Jones such purity.

The haematite, the iron oxide, red as the blood I would gladly have opened a vein of mine to spill a thousand times that I might have died in her place.

The jade, green as the morning grass where we walked that idyllic summer, through the silver birch wood where bluebells had grown that spring, where birds sang hosannas while church bells pealed 'they have found their love'.

The garnet, that hard glassy red silicate: how vividly I remember still the night it clung to her neck at the dance! How every woman was envious, and every man jealous. Now all I have is their pity.

The coral, as soft a red-pink as she turned at our first kiss: its properties have saved my house from storms, yet nothing can dispel the cloud that has hung over me for sixty years. Even my happiest moments since are tinged

————

with sadness that I spend them alone and at the memory of her last words: 'My only regret is that I must leave you.'

The turquoise, the green-blue of which reminds me of the burning summer sky when we first laughed, danced and sang like mad children. Never since has a day seemed worthy of celebration. How I tested the powers of this stone to the limit on my old horse that bitterly cold winter as if I could gallop away from reality.

The lapis, the midnight blue shot with a myriad of golden stars, makes me think of the place where my sweet Ophelia walks now, and of how my phoenix will never age: eternal youth is hers.

The amethyst, the violet quartz, Ophelia's favourite – and how we drank! Drank deeply from the cup of life, intoxicated with one another.

———

The pearl, the pale grey-white with a tinge of blue, the stone that brings a tear to my eye: it is the colour of her skin, and of the infant's too, as they lay forever in one another's arms. I knew that she would be taken from me when I dreamt of them, and many a tear has coursed my cheek since then.

The opal, the amorphous form of silicon dioxide, the jewel I hold to my lips, the one that lights my darkest hour: it is, as Pliny said, 'shadowed with the colour of wine'. When she wore it I called her Poederos. How she had then the beautiful complexion of youth: now she always will.

The diamond: its clear single purity is the love I still bear for my wife, but its qualities failed the somnambulist and the insane in me. For over half a century I have watched my once handsome countenance age in that same gilt mirror. Now it reflects an old, worn-out man as it once did a callow youth; dreaming now only of the day when once again I may experience the heaven above as I once did a heaven on earth.

The sapphire, the blue corundum, beloved of Saturn, god of greenery and vegetation: how its blue elates me! I press my lips to it as once I pressed them to the blue lips of Ophelia for the last time. Its quality of manly vigour, though, has failed me, for no vigour has coursed my veins from that day to this.

The emerald, the greenest beryl: how we loved the green and rolling pastures of Ireland and Wales, which sprang forth from it. We became one with the trees, the rivers, the ancient copses. But the qualities of this stone failed me too, and my child died, drawing but a single breath. And what venomous animal took Ophelia from me?

———

Each and every day I hold these gems, and each and every day, wonderful prismatic colours, that once shone so, grow dimmer. Often I see Ophelia's visage spring forth from them, and now she beckons. The lights grow dimmer still. Once again my Ophelia reaches for my hand; gently, tenderly, her youthful fingers take my aged arm. Once more I am with her; once again we will share the song and dance of soft, mad, laughing children.

————————

On a Clear Day

The moment Richard de Lorrain first set his eyes upon the ruined old house, he knew that he had to have it. An endowment had recently elevated him to a fairly affluent level; ample enough to fund both his literary and aesthetic aspirations and sensibilities. As he gazed at the house, he felt for the first time as if he were truly alive; his stillborn soul spluttered and gulped its first invigorating breath, burning as the life force surged through it. Every vein burned, every artery coursed with liquid fire, every pore lay open to a timeless, cleansing breeze that blew age upon age right through him.

'I must have it,' he murmured.

The old house had lain empty for many years. Like an aged Dickensian spinster, it seemed to have relinquished any claim to the present, and by simply doing nothing had become an anachronism. The years had rolled by. Some terribly brave youths had tried to blind her many years before but fled in a desperate panic when they heard the low agonised groan the house seemed to emit as the first stone shattered her panes.

More than any other he had ever seen, this house seemed to have a soul, an immense sad soul that lay dormant and abused somewhere deep within it. Her archaic countenance was shrouded in a century's neglect as ivy clamoured and clutched at it. The once warm and welcoming crunch of the paths and the beckoning and becoming guiles of the rose gardens lay overgrown with years of indifference.

———————

Everywhere the air hung thick with something almost tangible. It seemed to speak of the youthful belief, now turned sour, that love can change everything; the finality was that it had not changed anything at all. A natural yet preternatural demise seemed imminent, and only he, he felt, could offer salvation. He himself knew what it was like to set love in a position so elevated that the ideal could never be reached. Like every man who claims to have no ego, he still felt as though he were the one who could make the three-hundred-year wait of his prospective lover worthwhile.

'This is the one,' he thought to himself. It did indeed seem as if fate had brought the two tragic lovers together, to burn a scarlet oriflamme of consummation for their mutually first time. The peak had already been reached; the denouement would show the tragic flaws of both – a tragedy in which no one would learn a thing. How could they have known? How could they have avoided the scythe of destiny, even if they had had the knowledge to anticipate it? Sometimes we anticipate an approaching disaster but are still drawn to it, like an alcoholic to a bottle.

The house would be paradise for de Lorrain, both as a man and as a writer. He had the wealth to recreate an age long gone, recall a past he had never been privy to. Courtly love raised its chivalrous head. The older inamorata could teach and guide her new literary lover, and in return he, like an alchemist, would convert gall to manna, lead to gold. Only he could see the beauty lying dormant in the near-cadaverous abode he now gazed upon.

Over the coming months, many workmen moved to and fro, making efforts to beautify the old maid for her new lord. Intrusively they cleared the gardens and fixed the ponds, then started on the house. Meanwhile, de Lorrain made efforts to find out who had gone before him.

It was not long before his thirsty curiosities brought him to the cool oasis of the local archives. The house had been built in the early 1740s, almost a hundred and fifty years before. The first owner had felt uneasy about living there, and consequently never did break the maidenhead of his abode. For the first five years she had lain empty and intact, whilst her unfaithful paramour simply vanished. Rumours abounded that he had lost his sanity, but this was merely speculation. What was not speculation, however, was the knowledge that the house had been built on an Elizabethan burial mound acknowledged by many to have been used for invocations or other diabolical purposes; pagan rituals, tumescent orgies, and other acts of salacious and prurient carnality.

———————

25

He flushed as he read it. From his youth he had read de Sade and other such writers. Perhaps he had been drawn to this place by the same forces that had possessed them? Perhaps such forces would guide his pen into hitherto unexplored regions. He shook with anticipation.

Finally, at the end of 1894, the house was finished. The community of local tradesmen whom he felt to be stupidly superstitious did themselves no favours in his estimation when he heard them talking of cold chills in closed rooms, mists, groans, knocking, and a hideous laughing face. One even claimed to have heard screaming, but his was a solitary voice.

De Lorrain made arrangements to decorate the house before he could fully satisfy his pleasure. The uppermost storey first of all: a vast room, with leaded windows in each wall looking out onto the newly landscaped gardens. The walls were hung with Italian paper that proudly boasted upon it an opium poppy in full bloom. He began to fill the room with exotic plants of every hue and nationality, a large scrivener's writing desk, a pianoforte, a few chairs, some soft couches. Pictures by his favourite artists hung on the wall. When the soft glow of the chandelier was deemed too harsh, it was replaced by some old candelabra, which glowed red, thanks to their stained-glass surround. A menagerie of animals was moved in: jewelled tortoises crawled upon the floor; a large European mountain dog lay languorous and incongruous on oriental cushions. Snakes chosen for their colour lurked in the foliage. Beside a small pool basked salamanders and various small reptiles. Exotic shawls hung from ceiling to floor, imprinted with ethereal images of peacocks. Copper censers perfumed the air. A bust of Shelley and a bust of Byron stood on

either side of a great fireplace. All the furnishings were of soft, antiquated brass and
walnut. A drinks cabinet made from an old
pulpit served to highlight his rejection of religion. Amongst it all lay de Lorrain in an opium
and absinthe dream too fantastic for
description.

Though the rest of the house lay empty, the
fever of anticipation had grown so great that he
brought forward his wedding night to his new
bride, so eager were they both. The old four-
poster bed that lay in one corner, veiled with
heavy red velvet drapes that matched the
curtains, was first to know the young man's
restless soul as he retired. Sleep did not come
easy that night and as the hours passed he
decided to smoke a little hashish in order to
relax, to dull his fractured senses, for aside
from absinthe little alcohol passed his lips,
particularly wine and especially red wine.

Tenderly touched by the hands of an almost moribund torpor he smiled as he began to drift away in a dream of a magnitude only two new lovers could share.

Sometime later he awoke with a start. Even though he had shut off all the gaslights and enclosed himself in bloody red sensuality and crisp, white virginal linen a light still penetrated the warm safe sanctuary. Shouting voices and a drunken babble accompanied it. Slowly he parted the drapes and placed an eye to the split. The room seemed to be full of people. Scared and uncomprehending, he looked again. Sure enough, it was his room, but in the centre, from where the revelry emanated, it was devoid of furnishings save for a Hanoverian table and a few chairs.

———

The revellers seemed oblivious to him, so much so that the young aesthete became a little more brave and pulled the curtains apart a few more inches. The dangerous appeal which the house seemed to have previously held quickly coalesced. The actual danger was terrifying, however brave he considered himself. The thought of danger had merely alighted on his shattered equilibrium as a passing fancy. But now ...

Slowly his clouded perception began to clear and he was able to focus on the figures in front of him. Six men sat around the table gulping wine. At first, he had not recognised the clothes; bright muslin, embroidered coats not fashionable in a hundred and fifty years, full shirt sleeves, lace ruffles, breeches that only covered half the leg, round-toed shoes with a square silver buckle, powdered wigs pulled into a ponytail. But of the four characters who stood, two were only semi-clad, vying for the easy virtues of the four women who were present, all in various states of undress. Surely this could not be? De Lorrain, with mixed emotion, felt sure he recognised some members of the group. Was he really witnessing a gathering of the Hellfire Club?

The figures seemed to pulse, like a heartbeat; almost translucent they shimmered like reflections in a pool. Try as he might to discern voices, he could not. It was as if all those he observed were talking under water, water of a thick glutinous consistency that seemed to make every word last a century. But if his ears failed him, his eyes did not. He stared, stared in disbelief at what the assembled crowd appeared to be doing. Various tools of the occult were brought onto the table.

Suddenly, one of the crowd pointed directly at him, petrifying him. All the assembled faces

33

turned in his direction, and the man pointing proceeded to walk towards him. De Lorrain closed his eyes in dreadful anticipation. A cold chill fell right through him as the spirit walked through his. He turned, to see the figure standing on what appeared to be his bed, but to which the phantasm of a bygone age was obviously solid floor, as he was only visible from the waist up. Evidently, to him the bed simply did not exist, therefore neither did de Lorrain. The figure returned to his friends, carrying an old sack. De Lorrain began to laugh, first quietly then more loudly, hysterically. He leapt from the edge of the bed and rushed toward the group. He had made no conscious effort to will them here; perhaps that was why they could not see him. He touched one on the shoulder.

Flesh sliced spirit as easily as a rapier slices air. It was as if he were the ghost.

The gurgling language of the group fell silent as a skull with a pentagram carved on its forehead was removed from the bag and placed on the table. The cranial part was removed and red wine poured into it; all proceeded to drink. De Lorrain felt ill. Was this genuinely what had once happened in his room? Or was it all a product of his imagination, unlocked by the various hallucinogens he had imbibed throughout the course of the evening? Was it simply an elaborate plan the house had made in order to spurn him unequivocally?

As they all spread their palms on the table, making sure that the tips of their little fingers touched, one of the group seemed to fall into a trance. The room grew cold as the grave, as silent as a tomb. A window blew open and a howling gale entered. The table began to rock. A huge mound of earth violently erupted through the floor, throwing table, chairs and people in all directions. The small coven lay all about the room in disarray. As de Lorrain looked at the mound, there seemed to be movement from within it. With mounting horror he watched: three figures seemed to be emerging. Grime-covered, they struggled to the surface. Even more abstract than the first spectres in the room, these were certainly not the well-heeled affluent types, but peasants of the lowest rank, in the habiliments of the seventeenth century. Even though they were disgusting to look upon, one could sympathise: the former affluent group had no doubt used them for their sport. The poor and downtrodden would always be exploited in one way or another; some things do not change.

As he looked about him, de Lorrain realised with not a little surprise that he was the only

---

one who could see this new assemblage. One of them moved towards his affluent caller, and with icy hands clutched at his neck and began to squeeze. What was happening, de Lorrain mused – how could this be? A ghost killing a ghost! Or was it some kind of bend in time which afforded him the dubious honour of witnessing a murder of flesh by spirit, and which had made his house uninhabitable since the first days of its creation?

The invisible attacker continued to squeeze harder. Unable to see his assailant, the victim's gasps became desperate. Flailing and clutching his throat, he sought to peel away the invisible fingers that squeezed his life away, but the peasant tenaciously hung on. Finally, the deed was done. A corpse lay motionless, extinguished by a ghostly hand, the only witness to the perpetrator of the act a man born more than a hundred years after it had been committed.

Slowly the sun began to rise. The old house had never seemed so alive or so beautiful. The first rays of sunshine fell upon it. Finding a chink in the curtains of the old bed, they fell upon a dead body. Richard de Lorrain, aesthete, writer, dilettante and sometime property developer, lay lifeless. The crisp white linen sheets bore a stain instantly recognisable as that of red wine. Around his neck were numerous bruises, where an unseen hand had squeezed him away from life.

The Lake

Maxwell Wilkes looked at his watch. A quarter to midnight. Try as he might, he could not sleep. He was restless and anxious, brooding over a sense of guilt even he himself could not explain. The few grains of laudanum he had taken an hour previously had not helped. The room seemed to be closing in on him. He had suspicions that the drug had been tampered with, as he had obtained it from a chemist friend who was prone to playing such practical jokes. The Latin American drug Yage had been a talking point with them recently: perhaps it was this that now made the crimson hues of his heavy

---

embroidered curtains look like waterfalls of blood showering down the walls. His father's old bookcase took on the appearance of a coffin, what with the stained and crumbling tomes lining the shelves lying discarded like bones in a charnel house. Even the flames of his oil lamp appeared to be an exotic eastern dancing girl, beckoning him with flickering gyrations.

He had to escape. He broke into a sweat, yet was freezing cold. The room smelt musty and damp, sounds of Gregorian chants filled his head. His heartbeat became irregular, fluttering in his chest like an eagle in a canary cage, its wings breaking his ribs. What to do, what to do? Flee now, or stay and have all the evils of body and circumstances turn to bare slavering teeth on his flesh and sinews?

He lunged for the door. Opening it, he was in the passage, and staggered to the front of the house, the walls swirling. The figures in his beloved Pre-Raphaelite prints leered down at him from their frames. Pointing, they seemed to cry 'The hour is upon thee, satyr; death awaits thee, sybarite!' With voices ringing in his ears, he opened the heavy front door and took his first breath of the cold, midnight air.

He collapsed onto the grass. The cool dew on his face revived him, and after the oppressive heat of his opulent room the uncluttered chill of the night restored his senses somewhat. The mist clung to the earth, rising only a little over a foot off the ground, and as he looked about him, all that was visible to his eye was a deathly shroud that hung over his face like a veil.

He stood up. The clear sky and full moon made everything appear crisp and silent. He felt like an intruder in the stillness of it all. The only movement was that of the great trees, whose branches quivered like the limbs of a lover at the peak of ecstasy.

The huge lake at the bottom of the garden rippled with a silvery lustre, reminding him of his youth, days which seemed so distant now. How often, as a boy, he had swum in its loving embrace, before his father's tragic death, and long before the spectre of depression and neurasthenia had begun to plague his every waking moment. The demons that haunted him were now even tormenting his nights, depriving him of all but the briefest hours of sleep.

But now the lake seemed hostile, the only obstacle between himself and his sweet fiancée, Cynara. How he longed to hold her now, how he ached for her cool hands to wipe his brow and her soft kisses to ease the pain of living.

It was then he saw the small boat. It had not been used in five years, not since the death of his father, whom it was presumed had fallen from it one wintry morning, swallowed forever in the icy depths. Usually, Maxwell walked around the lake, even though it took a full hour, but with the boat he could be at Cynara's door in a quarter of that time.

Stealthily he made his way to the water's edge, checking his breathing as if the exhalations might wake his mother, she who had forbidden him ever to use the boat, keeping it as a shrine to her husband. The old lady still wore black, still mourned, worshipping Maxwell whose pale, dangerously wan appearance so mirrored that of the man she had married.

Maxwell untied the rope, stepped into the small wooden craft, fitted the oars into their mountings and pushed away from the shore. As silently as possible he began to row.

It was not long before the light of his room was obscured by the trees. Now there remained only the lake, the moon, the boat and the man.

———

43

On he rowed, pulling the oars deep into the water. The small boat skimmed across the surface. Why had he not thought to use it before? He laughed aloud at the thought of his pious mother finding the boat gone and imagining her husband had returned for his craft – a craft to row himself across the Styx, a craft of the living dead. He laughed again to think of all those who had seen his father's ghostly apparition at the water's edge, warning his kin to stay away from the lake and its mysterious depths, before emitting a death rattle and evaporating.

Maxwell stopped rowing. For one so unused to it, the physical exertion had already blistered his hands; those delicate pale hands which had never done a day's work. The boat drifted to a standstill. The moon cast a silvery shadow over the whole lake, illuminating it as brightly as would the midday sun. But however bright the sky, not one of its glowing fingers dared to penetrate more than a foot into the dank, murky waters.

Maxwell heard a sound. He glanced to his left. For a split second, he thought he saw a head disappear quickly beneath the waters a hundred or so feet away from him. Maxwell began to feel uneasy. No one knew how deep the lake really was, no one knew what undigested secrets lay in its intestines. Maxwell began to row again. Suddenly it was as if the boat had struck a brick wall. He quickly turned around as a half-human form sank into the waters, with the speed of a bullet yet without a ripple. The boat began rocking slightly; Maxwell spun around again, in time to see what appeared to be a giant slug slithering over the front of the boat. By the time his eyes were able to focus, he realised that it was a decomposing human arm. He let out a yell and hit it with an oar. The arm fell away at the elbow, and despite its wet putrefaction, the limb crumbled to dust. Maxwell sank into his seat, hardly believing what he had seen.

It was to be a brief respite. Within seconds, another arm slid over the side, then another, another, and another. Maxwell screamed! Whatever was on the end of the ghastly limbs could stay hidden. He lashed out as hard as he could, spinning and hitting. Then he caught sight of the lake. The whole of its surface bubbled and boiled with rotting corpses writhing over one another.

Maxwell flung himself into the bottom of the boat and closed his eyes. His mortality had never seemed so fragile. After what seemed an eternity, he opened them again, tentatively. Nothing had happened. He glanced up. Nothing. He stood up. The lake was perfectly calm.

Maxwell found his seat again. He was shaking. What had previously seemed a good idea now threatened to place his life upon a precipice. How he wished he were somewhere else, anywhere else!

Nervously he began to row. The small boat seemed to be gaining speed. Maxwell stopped rowing altogether; the speed of the craft's travel threatened to sweep him overboard. He glanced to the side. The water was no longer flat. He told himself that this defied the laws of physics, yet, if anything, the speed of the boat was increasing and the slope of the water steepening: ten-degrees, twenty-degrees, forty-degrees, sixty-degrees. Finally, the boat hit a ninety-degree angle and plummeted into free space. Maxwell looked above him. All he could see were the stars, beneath him only blackness. The waters moved to ninety-five degrees, and the little boat was engulfed.

———

The aqueous blackness infused his lungs, not with the texture of water but of adipocere. Its glutinous character filled every bronchiole. Maxwell closed his eyes and prayed for death.

When he reopened them, he was amazed. A myriad of sparkling colours hung all around him: bedazzling, swirling paisleys. He floated gently through the heavy, oily atmosphere; each new breath making the colours more majestic. Each one seemed to have its own light, an internal iridescence. It reminded him of the strange paintings of Gustave Moreau he had seen in Paris. Gently he drifted through the ever-changing waters. No solid forms appeared, all was bliss. Then blackness; for what seemed an eternity but was, in reality, a few brief seconds. A white light illuminated him from above, brighter than a thousand suns. Bathed in this limelight, Maxwell wondered who his audience was to be. In vain he squinted to his sides. In the dark recesses, vaguely discernible shapes made their appearance, then the uneasy feeling that all eyes were upon him. Suddenly he realised he was unable to move his body, only his head. His legs were hurting, and he glanced down. What he saw made him retch: his whole torso and both his legs were covered in leeches, oozing blood through their raw red skin–leeches with the faces of people, all with teeth buried deep in his flesh. Unable to move or speak, Maxwell felt his flesh shrivelling and desiccating.

It was then that he heard a voice, an awful, guttural voice, the voice of death, the voice of creaking hinges on a mausoleum door, a hoarse rasp from somewhere dark and unknown: a voice that burnt his skin as fiercely as the flames of Vulcan's forge. Maxwell narrowed his eyes into the gloom, trying to see whence or from whom the voice had emanated.

————

He wished he had not tried. A terrifying spectre was slowly slithering its way towards him, covered in the skin of a black and scaly reptile, with blood-red talons at the ends of its long bony fingers. It stood up in front of him, its constantly-squirming form barely contained by the rags that constituted its clothes. Rising to its full height, more than six feet above Maxwell, it slowly raised its hand to stroke the bone that pierced its skin where a chin should have been. Within the blink of an eye, the hand clutched at Maxwell's throat, as swiftly as a cobra strikes a mongoose. Raising Maxwell level with its blazing green eyes, the beast spoke. Squeezing his victim's throat, the great beast declared, 'Maxwell, through your love for me, I possess your soul.' Lack of breath, fright: whatever the cause, Maxwell slipped into un-consciousness.

When he awoke, he was back on the surface of the lake in his father's little boat. Everything was tranquil. He looked around him and all seemed truly at peace. He grabbed the oars and began to row, rowing as he never had before nor ever would again. His hands bled, his skin was soaking, his lungs raw and cold.

Soon he reached the other side of the lake. He sprang from the boat and ran. Soon he would be in Cynara's arms, soon all the pain would be gone. He knocked on the door. A light came on. The door creaked open and there stood the frame of his beloved Cynara, silhouetted against the soft glow behind her.

'Cynara, Cynara, I love you,' cried Maxwell, falling to her feet and kissing them.

'Maxwell, it's half past midnight,' said Cynara. 'Be quiet, or you'll wake Father.'

'I had to see you tonight,' said Maxwell. 'I love you more than life itself.' Maxwell knelt

———————

and gazed at Cynara's beautiful face. Tonight, though, it seemed different. He had seen her face a thousand times before, but he had never realised just how green were her eyes.

'Oh, Maxwell,' said Cynara, 'you and your love! I truly think you would lose your soul to love…'

———

A Thing of Beauty is a Joy to Behold

A ubrey Cain was unhappy. There had been no external event to trigger the emotion, but the period of convalescence he had spent at his parents' had afforded him the time to analyse his concepts of existence and mortality, and the conclusion he had come to had been a surprise to him. Of course, the illness had inevitably clouded and coloured his perspectives, but try as he may, the memory of ever having felt any different had been dismissed: he had always felt this way, but had never had the time to actually think about it before. The conclusion drawn he felt to be a just and honest one.

Immortal longings dwelled within him that yearned to escape and wander barefoot in the cool green grass, caressed by a gentle warm breeze. Somewhere there were golden pastures hidden from the eyes of man, where one could live in a state of perpetual bliss, where the sobbing violins of Autumn would never give way to the frigid, frozen principality of which he found himself a prince, and which he so loathed. But where existed such a place? Certainly no one known to him knew the way there or even recognised that such a place existed.

Aubrey's longings were tolerated. Some even recognised that he was a hopeless dreamer whose feeble frame had wandered in a Gethsemane garden but who had sold his fragile state of mind for thirty pieces of silver.

In the middle of April, Aubrey was able to leave his sickbed for the first time in many,

---

many months. Ennui had manifested itself of late, and now each step was tortuous with wasted limbs quickly tiring. The collusion between mind and body was doubly debilitating. Aged less than thirty, yet what seemed left? The tallow-white skin, as taut as a child's, seemed to crease a little at the prospect. Age, he realised, would wither him, and custom stale.

From the verandah he had watched the many trees in his father's garden, in the harsh, cold winter when their stiff appendages had penetrated the sky, tearing huge gashes into it; their stark limbs crowned in thorns, stiff as a cold corpse, awaited the resurrection which was now beginning to take place. The new spring sun eased apart the wedding-white blossom, which reciprocated the warm caresses. The occasional red berry, like a small spot of blood, was to be expected among the innocent flowering. The product of the union,

---

shadows spattered and then swam in haphazard form on the new wet grass, eventually to fall in the shallow pebbled stream that carried them away in a constant purifying souse.

As the scene before him filtered through and eventually nailed itself to the walls of his mind, it seemed at last that the progenitive quality had not been totally curtailed: the immortal longings he had had for so many years began to respond, the two coming together in a process of fertilisation that made him shake and sweat. The lifeblood that coursed in every vein and artery, which for so long had seemed in decay, now swelled every limb in tingling ecstasy. His vision, the transcendent nature of that vision of which he had been a part, for the first time gave him the knowledge, so arcane, to stand outside himself. Others could seek escape or even oblivion; he had found a private, secret salvation, a personal shrine at which he alone could worship.

Over the following weeks, the happiness within him became more and more apparent. The locals still recognised him as the hopeless dreamer who 'hadn't a good day's work in 'im'. It was with a mixture of pity, sympathy and patronising superiority that they did so – ennobling reasons which they felt gave them a charitable disposition: it made them feel good to think themselves better than one person in this world, at least. As a priest views his congregation, it was with a feigned benevolence that they viewed the 'poor wretch'. Never was a soul so worthy of redemption!

With the insight his present circumstances afforded him, Aubrey seemed oblivious to it all, wandering in the garden, a fixed smile on his face as he gazed into the tumescent limbs of the trees. Occasionally, words of reverence and awe spilt forth almost unconsciously.

The weeks passed, but the family's pleasure had a serpent in it. The ghostly pallor of their son remained, and his mother especially found it disconcerting to see the white skin, almost translucent and seeming to radiate with an inner light, pressed against the lower branches of the tree, the pinkish-white of the blossom the only thing that gave her son any semblance of a living man. A dream also upset her. She worried: what would happen when the blossom went? The effect the soft petals had upon her son she knew to be a transient one. Their beauty would be ephemeral, fleeting. They had arrived in a state of beauty, existed in a state of beauty would die that way. However much her son loved them, their beauty could not be captured, absorbed or held in any way at all, however much one might wish to do so.

———————

One day, from his window, Aubrey saw the branches of the trees quiver as a light breeze passed through them, and, in a state of stupefied reverence, he watched as thousands upon thousands of the petals fell from the canopy, tearing tiny holes in the shroud. Like confetti, they fell, carpeting the floor. The whole vision turned white. Like a gentle fall of snow, it fluttered to earth in silent, resigned decay, still as beautiful as the day he had first seen it. Quickly he dressed and ran outside, hoping to be an intrinsic part of what he saw.

Cool and gossamer-like, the petals stuck to his bare hands, feet and face as he availed himself to the deluge. His familiarity with all that lay before him stripped him of any incongruity now bare and naked, he proffered himself as a sacrificial lamb before the altar of all that he loved or would ever love.

———

A THING OF BEAUTY

The petals continued to float slowly down as if the air had a certain viscosity for them, contrasting radically with the light and refreshing nature of the heady balm Aubrey imbibed. He fell to his knees and lifted petals by the handful, bathing himself in their nature, smell, every quality they had, every quality he held dear and wished he himself possessed.

Slowly the breeze stopped, and the petals' last journey also fluttered to an end. Aubrey stood up. Tiny petals stuck to his hands and feet. After a few moments of dumb celebration he brushed them off, but none moved. A little harder this time, yet all stayed as they were when they had landed. With growing alarm and consternation, he tried to peel one off, but the pain was excruciating. With disbelief he saw that the rending of it had drawn blood, which rose to the fullness of the wound, obeyed the laws of gravity and followed a course to the end of his finger, whence it dripped to the white floor. For such a delicate constitution the stark contrast between the deep red and the pink-white was frightening to behold.

In a daze, he ran to the edge of a small pool which the stream in the garden constantly flushed with fresh waters. In frozen animation, he gazed at his reflection on the silver smooth surface. An inverted Narcissus, the sight was hateful to him. A transfiguration had taken place. The flesh tone of the petals had stuck fast to his own; every inch of what was visible was covered in tiny gossamer scales. Beauty, and the search for it, had begotten a monster!

Hearing his mother's voice calling him, he began to panic. He caught a glimpse of her blue dress, though she had not yet seen him. How could he let her see him like this? His mother had always seemed to him so unsullied, uncorrupted – now to have to witness the punishment which had been meted out to her son for crimes he had not committed. Thinking him gone to the local town, she went back inside the house. Aubrey realised that, until some cure could be found for the way he now looked, he must remain out of her sight. But what he had sought and acquired was now a part of him, and to try to divorce it from himself would take a fundamental change in his entire outlook on life. Uncomprehending of any whys or wheres, all Aubrey realised was that what lay ahead of him was incomprehensible. It would be a permanent cross he would have to bear.

Taking a few apples from a nearby building, still replete with autumn's harvest, Aubrey planned to leave, to contemplate his predicament. Stepping out into the road, he had gone but a short distance when he heard voices and, from a corner, a few small children appeared. At first, they did not seem to notice Aubrey's reptilian disfigurement – after all, the petals had the tones of flesh – but as they neared him, his scaly appearance caused them to stare, at first with intrigue, then with fear. Formerly the local children had been more tolerant of Aubrey than had their parents; if this was the effect which he now had upon them, what then would be the effect on their parents?

The staring children's lips began to quiver, and their eyes, like flooded pools, flushed the plains of their cheeks. With equal disgust, Aubrey realised that this would now forever be his lot in life: branded with the mark of Cain. What had once been beautiful had made a pariah of him. It was incomprehensible to him; how could he hope others comprehend? The transfiguration was complete. He could never return.

―――――――

'Would you like an apple?' Aubrey said to them in an effort to return them to their natural selves. With trepidation, two tiny hands stretched forward and quickly stole forth the gifts. Turning away, the two corrupted innocents stumbled and fell.

Aubrey sat down on a low wall. He wept. As if in sympathy or rage, the grey sky above him made a fearful crack and began to rain.

A Day in the Life of Abraham Marainein

braham Marainein looked in the mirror. He felt old. Every day he would gaze at his countenance in one of his many mirrors, for his greatest pleasure was his own reflection. But today was different. Despite being only twenty-six, he could feel the qualities of youth he had once possessed slipping through his hands like water. He had a sophistication and an erudition far beyond his years, and they made him appear older than he actually was. The only incongruous factor was his face: black ringlets framed a bone structure of which any woman would have been proud, and large dark eyes flashed

---

beneath eyebrows that gave his expression a permanently cynical aspect; nonetheless, his face still had an androgynous quality betrayed only by dark stubble.

Abraham allowed himself a rare smile. He knew he was handsome, he knew women found him irresistible, and that his effect on men was often the same. All acknowledged, he felt, that they were in the presence of a superior being. They squirmed, fawned upon and pampered the vain young man, anxious to win his favour and to bask in a reflected glory, whilst he observed, impenetrable and aloof.

To all intents and purposes, Abraham had everything. His father had died when Abraham was thirteen, leaving him the prospect of one day becoming a wealthy man. He knew he would never have to work, and he had never intended to: 'Work is the scourge of the drinking classes,' a friend had once said to him.

————

But for all that his good fortune had brought him, his wealth had not bought him happiness. He was painfully aware that his needs were infinite, the possibility of his pleasures finite. Nothing satiated his needs. His search for that elusive something tormented him like an unquenched thirst. Constantly he felt the need to experience more. He had realised long ago that money could not buy it; he had also realised that without it he could not survive. His appearance became his only pleasure. Nothing mattered except the glorification of his sensual pleasures.

The previous year, he had decided to furnish his new house. He sought to worship in the temple of his eyes and travelled to France to buy some prints and soak up the atmosphere of aestheticism that he had heard so much about and which so suited his temperament.

He bought a self-portrait of Bocklin, with death in the wings. Whilst he stayed at the Hotel de Ville he saw some Clairin, buying a print of *The Distant Princess*; *Satan's Treasure* by Jean Delville, as much for the name as for the print; a Ferdinand Keller, some Khnopffs, a Karel Masek; a dozen cases of champagne for the Mucha labels; *The Sphinx* by von Stuck; a beautifully framed *Corner of a Room* of the poets Rimbaud and Verlaine by Fantin-Latour. How his heart filled! His desire for the perverse, for the symbolic, had been satisfied. His longing to escape reality had been animated in these beautiful paintings; for once the world seemed a glorious place. The immortality of those canvases contrasted so sharply with the transience of his fading youth. How he longed to escape to another time, another place, where the amaranth of his lost adolescence would bloom once again.

———————

But, oh! How briefly those paintings had filled the void. Back in the grimy streets of London, full of grimy people, he soon felt alone again – even in a crowded room he felt alone. He observed the human race as a scientist observes amoeba under a microscope. He went out to observe; often he went out simply to make his superior presence known. He went to the theatre, of course: Debussy, Ravel, Satie and the lost soul opera of Wagner. All demanded a certain dress: the right colour gloves, carnation, walking cane, perfumes. One could never wear black to Ravel, nor viridian to Wagner.

Yes, today was different. He felt his once-handsome face to be ageing, and he was afraid that if his youth should die then so would he. His house, like his appearance, had become a shrine to the perverse, but his house had taken perversity to new heights: every room had been decorated in a single colour. As his mood was black, he went to his black room.

A huge ebony-framed mirror hung majestically opposite the door. Erotic black and white prints by a strange friend of his clung to the wall like specks of blood coughed from the diseased lungs of the consumptive. Abraham moved toward his chair, across the huge black rug that lay in wait in front of the fire. Rows of jars filled with preservative and medical school oddities lined the shelves. Money could buy anything, Abraham reflected. Rows of books lay on other shelves, all covered in black reptile skin, so as to be in harmony with the rest of the room. To have them covered in such a manner had cost him as much as it would have taken an ordinary man a full year to earn, but no matter. They were pleasing to his eye, and nothing else came into consideration.

Abraham sat down. The heavy black bro-
cade curtains and black lace at the window
subjugated the midday sun, rendering the
room a constant half-twilight. He lit a row of
black candles in order to read and picked up a
book: a collection of eroticism that a poet friend
had given him. How often as a younger man he
had read its depravities agog! Now they bored
him. His life of dissipation had intertwined
fantasy and reality to a point of uncertainty as
to whether he had read the book and imagined
the acts or committed the acts and written
about them himself. Did the world now hold
any secrets for him? Had every pleasure been
drunk to the very last quaff? Was this reality all
there really was?

He slammed the book shut and closed his
eyes. He yearned to escape reality, to run away
to a happier place. In his blacker moments he
wished he were someone else, but the thought

that he would not then be himself depressed him all the more.

He stood up and went to the mirror. It was time for a change. Abraham needed once again to brave the lonely London streets. A new play was opening this evening, and he made up his mind to go.

Although Abraham was certainly a misanthrope, it was a peculiar paradox of his character that, possibly to seek some excitement for his surfeit of sensibilities, he would always walk to where he wished to be, often taking a deliberate detour through the rough, run-down areas that one would suppose to be anathema to him; but like those addicted to the Gothic novel, he sought the sublime experience through terror.

Abraham set out quite early with just such a detour in mind. How he hoped that the evening would reanimate some passion with a

---

74

jolt to the jaundiced equilibrium that he had become too apathetic to even disturb, let alone dispel.

As the area of Highgate where he lived gave way to the more working-class environs to the east, he felt a slight adrenalin surge shoot through him. This, he knew, was a dangerous area. Many murders had been committed there some years previously by a man dubbed 'Jack the Ripper'. He knew the locals had suspected a 'gentleman' of these deeds. With his sartorial elegance, he knew he ran the risk of attack and the possibility thrilled him.

Eventually, he found himself within White-chapel, having taken a hansom cab to save his legs the exertion of such a prolonged detour. He stepped out of the cab and paid the driver. The air hung heavy with claustrophobic oppression, and it was not long before he became aware that he was being followed. A delicious sense of his own distress ran through him as he continued to walk. The footsteps grew nearer. There were two pairs, or was it three? Excited by his own vulnerability, he was nevertheless startled when a hand clasped his shoulder.

'Hello then, Miss. Not from round this way, are you? Lost your way?' said a Bow Bells voice. Abraham did not answer.

'Well well, it's a fella!' his aggressor said, with as much sense of irony as his narrow mind could muster. His friend could just grunt with grinning approval.

'But a pretty one!' he continued. Abraham's heart pounded. The realisation of his fantasy struck fear into him, but still it was strangely exciting.

'Give us a kiss then, pretty,' said the sca-brous individual who held him. And with that, he forced his lips against Abraham's. With in-

---

creasing salaciousness, he forced his tongue between the tightly closed lips. Abraham bit, an act he recognised as either heroic or stupid. Biting harder, he felt his teeth meet, and blood flowed into his mouth and gushed down his throat.

'Aah, he bit me!' the man screamed, in words ill-expressed due to the absence of half his tongue; blood, like a fountain, poured from his mouth.

Taking advantage of the confusion and panic, Abraham ran, ran as fast as he could. Hailing a hansom cab, he leapt into it. Only then could he consciously think of what had just happened. What had he found so invigorating? Was it the thought of placing himself in an alien environment? Was it the thought of laying himself open to physical attack? He found the thought of both painfully pleasing. But the more he thought about it, the more the

---

same conclusion became apparent. The climax of pleasure had come in the taking of another's blood! His aristocratic English frame gave a shudder, yet slowly he allowed himself a smile. The life force of another was the one thing his money could not buy, but the taking of it he now knew would be his new pleasure, his new vice, his new compulsion!

How My Father Taught Me to Hate Myself

As the curtains peeled apart and the wooden box trundled away towards its final destination, the solitary soul allowed himself the luxury of a few moments' silent reflection.

The heat of the day was suffocating; nowhere was there a breath of wind. Everywhere the air hung heavy with a clammy, tactile quality that coiled around him like a constricting serpent.

The heat made any great display of emotion tiring ... tedious, but the observer was not in the mood for emotion anyway; everything seemed so distant, unreal. Instead, he remained

---

aloof, calm in his disposition, even though it was his father who was being cremated. To become involved in any capacity would be far too strenuous, and would make him a hypocrite. Even the flies seemed listless. The room was as silent as the grave. Everything had a hazy timelessness which afforded the indulgence of reflection, and he wallowed in it.

Death is queer, life a strange phenomenon. What makes a lump of bone, blood, muscle move and act of its own accord? What force leaves it upon death, at once allowing the hideous processes of putrefaction to take a hold in its place? Putrefaction. Wasn't it Rousseau who said 'We are born of our Mother's bloodied entrails, and end in a mass of putrefaction'? Why? The process of conception, life, death – all a mystery beyond com-prehension. How alarmed would we be if the power, the 'will' that animates matter, could be

_____

caught, captured, introduced to inanimate things, or even re-introduced to flesh that lay devoid of it? What agonies would a lamb chop go through if the life force could be restored to it? He allowed himself a smile as he thought of his father as a giant lamb chop. But this heat ... it really was beginning to become unbearable.

Thoughts of life and death once again returned to him. How easily life could be snuffed out! The human form, like a perfectly sealed piece of fruit, could be destroyed just as easily with the introduction of a strategically aimed blade. Native Americans had seen mortal wounds inflicted on cold days and noticed steam emitting as the warm blood hit the cold air, supposing it to be the soul escaping. Perhaps it was.

Death. The notion of it was not a straightforward black or white. Different deaths have different values. A listless fly lethargically

---

landed on his hand: he crushed the life from its fragile body. He felt not the slightest twinge of remorse or regret; just as the death of his father had failed to shatter his sangfroid. He yawned. Both deaths, he recognised, had been the culmination of futile lives. What had the fly achieved with its life? What had his father? Who would remember either of them? He was now the only being who remembered his father and with his death there would be nothing to show that the old man had ever existed. Not only was his life fragile, then; it was transient ... ephemeral.

The heat of the day elicited such reflections. He had been allowed the afternoon off, so the rest of the day was his own possession. He closed his eyes and slipped back into reverie. It really was so hot ... the realisation went through his whole body like a pulse, a small electric shock.

Values of life came into his mind. How hypocritical we are! He detested blood sports but for the first time his critical eye landed on those, like himself, who opposed it. How many of this band, with no qualms or guilt, would poison vermin if found in the same abode as themselves? Why was a rat's life of less value than that of a fox? If one is to oppose death, one must oppose all deaths, without discrimination. But how successful is opposition? Death still comes like a tenacious, unrelenting affliction to everyone and everything. Why? What systems come into operation to bring about such a shutdown?

All our lives we assume we control our bodies, but the final reality to be recognised is that we lie paralysed and trapped within a fleshly prison, as surely as his father was enclosed in the box in which he now lay.

When the body takes a decision, independently of the will, to make the unique and final shutdown, the will is powerless to say no. The unity we have always considered our very selves is thrown into disarray. The chasm between will and corporeality becomes unbreachable ... an immeasurable chasm separates the two. Flesh aligns itself to the will's enemy, death. The two join forces and destroy their own dominion.

A hot wave coursed through him once again. What could be done to escape it? To escape anything? In a world of chaos, some things may seem preordained. We know there will be hot days; we know we will die. We know that in the final months, weeks, days, moments of our 'life' the will, recognising defeat, loses its ability to make order of this chaos, recognises the futility of existence and embraces religion in the vain hope of obtaining

84

a second chance; or worse, in the hope of some eternal reward in appreciation of many years of self-abnegation – well, sometimes.

Should we avoid action we deem to be wrong? Why? No law of ethics exists in Nature. It was just another example of the frightened little lamb, Man, creating repressive values to govern his own behaviour, to compartmentalise everything, to destroy his natural beauty and stay within the confines of what we deem to be good and evil.

Are we really shut away and entirely independent of one another as one planet is from another? All shut away in our little boxes. Never knowing when the flesh that surrounds us will say 'it's time to die'. Never knowing what anyone else is thinking. Religion is the last recourse of the desperate: human life, mysterious and incomprehensible; human beings, frightened hypocrites, desperately latching on

───────

to any prospect of salvation offered them yet created by them!

Suddenly he smelt burning and opened his eyes. Everything was black. The heat was rising. He could feel his blood boiling like sauce in a saucepan, and like that sauce, thickening and congealing. He tried to stand but hit his head. Reaching out, he felt his confines: a small box. The burning he recognised as the box in which he was trapped! His box, with him inside it, was about to be consumed by flames. Not his father's cremation after all, but his own. Like a lamb to the slaughter, he had come in innocence to his own annihilation, uncomprehending. His death was upon him. A million hushed harsh whispers seemed to be saying 'burn, burn', and as the first flames broke through the scorching panels, he spoke for the first time: 'God ... I still deny you.'

And as we walked away from the charred re-
mains of the funeral pyre, we all agreed: how
dare anyone think such thoughts! An affront to
the accepted order of things ... like all anom-
alies and freaks, it was his destiny not to thrive:
it would be foolish to think otherwise.

From the Blood of Innocence

Carpathia

31st December 1899

My dear Victoria,

I can scarcely bring myself to articulate my feelings on the written page, but try I must. Rejoice, my love! Information has come to me that confirms what I had always hoped.

Many arcane artefacts have recently been acquired in a trunk I bought in an auction. The superstitious locals shied away from it and it was mine for a song. Many of the books we had always looked for were in it: "Philosophicae et Christianae Cogitationes de Vampires" from 1733 by De Schertz, Mannhardt's "Ueber Vampirismus" in Volume IV of "Zeitschrift für Deutsche Mythologie", which was also very old. But best of all, a Sylvanite cross, a large splinter of wood and three nails, the relevance of which will soon become apparent to you.

Many manuscripts were enclosed; a few, with the artefacts that I have already mentioned, were written in an ancient language I have been endeavouring to understand and translate, and the monumental knowledge they impart is all that we have ever dreamed of. What follows is my rather stilted translation.

⌣

At the beginning of the first millennium there walked two men, two opposite men, as opposite as day and night. One was divine to look upon. Beauty radiated from his features. He had many admirers, and on the dusty roads of Nazareth and Jerusalem, many base men told of the transformation he had wrought upon their dark souls.

The other was repulsive. Propagated by the first serpent, he was born of a fallen woman, and his countenance struck fear into the heart of all who dared to look upon him. Many were afraid and forced him from their midst. He wandered as an outcast.

Through an accident of birth, the first was born for eternal paradise in the kingdom of his father; the second was born for eternal purgatory, hidden away in the dark forests of Central Europe.

But as the obverse sides of a coin are intrinsically forged, so were these two men. The first bore no ill will or hatred, for he was incapable of it. The second, after many years of ostracism, became bitter as wormwood and gall, seeking revenge on those he blamed for his state; and by the forces of darkness,

---

he propelled himself to the land of the first, to seek revenge. And as the first serpent tempted Eve with thoughts previously unknown to her, the second, through the terror of his countenance, planted an evil seed in the fertile, weak minds of those that he met, turning their bitterness against the first man, though he was as Nazarene as they.

The second supplied the thirty pieces of silver to his father's servant: the Nazarene was betrayed, tried and condemned. Three

nails he wrought upon his father's anvil,

which he supplied to his collaborators.

Selecting a site where the first serpent's foul

deed had gone awry, he sought sweet revenge

by seeking to emulate his father's crime.

Adam's tree was duly planted in the

shade of two others, and the Nazarene nailed

to it. The blood of innocence that flowed gave

the evil one cause to rejoice, and the life spilt

over his upturned face. He drank, in the hope of gratifying his own ends.

After a few hours, he fell ill. The colour drained from his face, the flesh seemed to fall from his bones, the whites of his eyes became broken and red, and the nails on his hands became like the talons of animals that prey on the weak. The former wretchedness of his countenance doubled. Even nature fell silent, seemingly leaving a gap in its effort to avoid any contact with the fatal wanderer.

Morning came with a light so painful to him

that he had to hide himself away. But as

night fell, two visitations came unto him: first

an angel, then a messenger of darkness, a

daemon.

The angel spoke to him: " For your

sins, your appearance shall forever remain as

it is now. Your flesh will always betray the

corruption to which you have stooped. As you

have taken the blood of immortality, so it shall now forever remain with you. Never again shall you feel the warmth of light on your back or know the joy or possibility of friendship. For all eternity you are condemned to inhabit only darkness, utterly alone. No man shall ever suffer the pain that your appearance will elicit."

The man began to repent his actions and begged forgiveness, but the angel had gone.

After a few hours, the daemon appeared and spoke.

"Fear not, your salvation has come. The course you have chosen to follow, none have walked. We salute you and crown you with a crown of thorns. As you drank the blood of innocence, so you committed your mortal house to decay without end. But you can be saved. As you drank the blood of innocence once, so you must again. But just as the first blood of innocence corrupted, all from now on will restore. The power to gratify your desires will always be with you."

And so it was that the man fled the hot and arid lands whose sun scorched his skin, and sought the land from which he came, and the dense forest. The Antichrist is in our midst. Just as the daemon had promised, the innocence of his victims restores his countenance and with each new victim he is more divine to look upon, though with each infusion he grows paler – legend has it, as pale as Seneca's widow. The victims usually live, but their life force quickly dissipates and they are robbed of their treasured vitality. Occasionally atheists are chosen, and their transformation is frightening: they become one with the perpetrator of the crime committed against them.

No weapon can destroy him, save the

ones he himself possesses: a splinter from the bough of the cross, the three nails which held the Nazarene upon it, and a crucifix cast from the ore of his homeland.

Is this truly more than we could have hoped for? My theories as to the origins of the vampyre were true. His immortality was stolen from the blood of Christ! And the only reliques that can destroy him are in my possession!

Believe in him, V. Pray to him, revere his countenance. He alone will rid our lands of pestilential Christianity. He is among us!

But I must conclude. Thoughts of him have debilitated my spirit, and I grow ever more weak. In spirit, he comes to me yet, and I rejoice. My misanthropy grows ever more acute; only this can alleviate it. We shall be reborn through a baptism of blood! Through every dark day in history he has been present! V., we can be there too! Eternity is in our lips and eyes, just a breath away. Let the beating wings of daemons cool your brow as they cool mine. Only by the distillation of evil shall we have immortality.

I urge you to come at once. Nothing can part us once we have the secret of his arcane immortality. And with the reliques I hold, I am in the perfect position to bargain for an imparting of it. Come to me!

I am and remain

Yours ever lovingly

A.

All a Dream

As the burning embers turned to ash, an eruption from its midst took place; from it, a giant golden phoenix emerged and bade me ride upon its back. Its silver and golden lustre, beaten to gossamer thinness, was as soft as a bed of magnolia petals; I slipped into the gentle arms of Morpheus.

On awaking, I found myself in a strange new and wonderful land. All colours were painfully pleasing in their brilliance. The cool green grass beneath my feet shone, as each heavy blade stood crowned with a heavy dewdrop suspended in eternal animation like a glutinous gem.

A river that flowed nearby sang like a host of angels laughing. Its bubbling torrent, like liquefied diamonds, sparkled and shone before my eyes, its crystal clarity showing cool soothing depths.

From the trees came the sounds of harps and flutes, their delicate leaves sanctified every time the sigh of a perfumed breeze fell upon them.

As I walked, tentatively at first – for such beauty was unknown to me – the path that carried me into the wood seemed to shimmer beneath my feet. The lustrous canopy that shielded my eyes from the startling cerulean sky occasionally yielded to it, and a brilliant bright blue sky burst forth to kiss and caress my face, which, upturned, was cooled by the beating wings of ethereal and celestial cherubs.

———

Many strange animals passed before me in the silent still centre of this sylvan scene. I spied a pool like that of a transfixed tear on the face of a false idol. From it drank a unicorn, wondrous in its wedding whiteness. As I gazed, its powerful wings lifted it airborne and away from me. Far into the distance it flew, to alight on an island in the middle of a lake that shone in mother-of-pearl magnificence, as both Phoebus beamed peace and warmth and the sovereign of true melancholy graced and garlanded all I saw before me in that unified moment that is both day and night.

My phoenix returned and took me to the shores of this beauty. The heady balm of orchids and lilies, almost intoxicating, filled me with exaltation and joy. Ten thousand lily leaves rained upon me, gilding a path to the palace, whose entrance was the gateway to paradise. Inside, strange trees grew with

---

strange fruit, a gift from Zeus and his minions. Music infused every part of me, sparkling colours radiated before me.

The walls of the palace had mortar made with the juice of jasmine and frangipani. Warm aromatic zephyrs blew through me, cleansing, permeating the fresco walls that were painted in a hand that was to Raphael's as Raphael's was to a child, extending eternally in every direction, furnished in Alexandrian splendour. From the cathedral-high ceiling swung censers. All around were staircases carved from every imaginable gemstone, all gleaming with an inner light.

Climbing a nearby staircase that led to an array of stained glass windows, seemingly crafted at the dawn of creation, I spied the world without. One lancet arch was empty, the glass fractured and broken. I turned to it, so that my eyes might adore all that I saw, but was aghast at what befell them.

From the window, mortality lay about me in chains; children and animals beaten for no sin or crime; I witnessed the ugly face of intolerance; countries divided and wartorn; lives condemned to frailty through want; many starving whilst others grew fat; people living lives they felt had no purpose or reason. All I saw, yet none saw me. None broke their fetters and manacles to look with the inward eye that gives the lonely a friend and the prisoner freedom.

And so I choose my course: oblivion from it all ...

The Sins of the Fathers

The scrap of humanity no one had expected to live had now matured into a young man, against all the odds. His existence was still painful and traumatic, however, and would always be so. His father beheld the affliction his son had with disdain, feeling it a slight on his virility. The religious side of his character permeated his every thought and action; any sexual liaison therefore was felt to be accursed and sinful. Before him walked the result of religious justice, and he felt such results to have been a fair execution. His mother, though, loved her only son and had taken a vow never to bless him with a sibling, as such a child might well turn out to be like the monster her husband felt their firstborn had been.

No one knew the exact cause of young Edward Gray's affliction. Medical science had called it Porphyria. Laymen would just consider his appearance as too frightening to look upon. His terrible affliction cursed his every waking moment. Less unhappy times were spent in the hours of darkness when the sun's painful rays were safely hidden and the agonising beams could not avail themselves of his bleached countenance. In darkness he could rest easy without the constant threat of pain coursing through his body. His bloodshot eyes could only focus after the midnight hour when the constant threat of nature's flame being thrust into their midst had disappeared. But no time, day or night, could cicatrise his easily cracked and ever-bleeding skin. He felt himself

———

accursed, and like all accursed things, felt it his duty to hide himself away from society; a society that would reject him, and whose rejection he reluctantly felt bound to reciprocate. Old wives' tales circulated in the village about 'the living corpse', many believing he did not exist. Others thought him a curse, the result of some profane and illicit union many years before. It had not helped when the local doctor, a thoroughly disreputable type, had made a drunken diagnosis, the result of hearsay, and had diagnosed Porphyria, proudly stating incest as the root cause. The misery such gossip had engendered within the thoroughly upright and pious family was untold. The wisp of affection the parents still bore was withdrawn still further. They felt the right decision now would be to confine their son forcibly to the most ancient and remote part of the large estate

———————

which they called home, but which for him would now become a prison.

The confines of his small quarters, though well-furnished in the decor of the day, quickly became tedious and hideously monotonous. The young man, due solely to his lack of companionship, came more and more to rely on his imagination as the sole form of escape. The waking moments of every day were spent in guilt and torment, yet lost in a reverie of far-off places he had seen in his father's books and of the people who had once inhabited such lands. With a sigh of resignation, the ideas were shut away into the realms of fantasy, with the realisation that physical escape would always lie intangibly out of reach. His physical circumstances bound him, as surely as poverty and lack of education bound the poor but healthy inhabitants of the local towns. His restrictions were of a different form but just as constricting and debilitating to wellbeing; one could either lie down and let life crush the desire to enjoy it - like an old cider press crushes little apples - or if circumstances are insurmountable, divorce oneself from reality and create a personal world, free from pain, irritation and the hurt a thoughtless world of fellow man can cause.

The oppressive gloom of his room would have hung heavy over most spirits, like a damp shroud, but his condition rendered the obliteration of any light necessary. A few candles that were the only illumination lent the ancient room an archaic air, though its modern Edwardian decor paradoxically gave it a very contemporary feel. It was doubly ironic in that it would have done any fashionable young man about town very proud indeed. He, however, sought to escape. Closing his eyes, he dared to dream; soon sleep crept over him.

After a brief lapse of time, he awoke. The room stood bathed in glorious sunlight, causing the now instinctive gesture of covering his eyes. After a few seconds there was a realisation: this time there had been no pain, this time was different. He opened his eyes and looked around. It was certainly still the same room, only the decoration and furnishings had changed entirely. Gone was the furniture of his period: the whole room was now decorated in what appeared to be the style of the Jacobean age. Gone was his brass bed; he was now in a four-poster affair. The paintings which had hung on his walls, depicting the fashionable world of Paris and London, had been replaced by tapestries of bucolic scenes. The smooth white walls of his room were gone, to be replaced by rough stone. He ran to the window. The familiar rolling lawns of his father's estate were still there but were now scattered with innumerable rose bushes and a small stone fountain.

Voices in the passage caused him to panic. The door opened and in walked what appeared to him, in his limited experience, to be the most beautiful girl in the world.

'Hello, you must be my cousin back from Spain,' she said, half-jovially, half-teasingly. 'Mother has told me so much about you, I feel as though I know you already.'

'Yes,' he murmured hesitantly, faltering and not knowing what to say to this apparent stranger who appeared to know him. He gazed at her as she flitted to the window, babbling garrulously words he had ceased to take in. Her clothes were not the fashion of his era. Her hairstyle, everything about her, was of a different age. Her delicate hand ran over a tapestry she was doing: 'Elizabeth Wheatley, age 16, August 1615'. Sixteen fifteen! With total incomprehension, he realised that somehow he was living, breathing, moving almost three hundred years earlier than when he had gone to sleep.

'Come with me, John,' the young woman said, 'Let me introduce you to my brothers and sisters.'

'John?', he thought but said nothing. They left the room together, his gut twisting itself into knot upon knot in dread and anticipation. Why hadn't his face frightened her? Why didn't his eyes hurt? What would her family say when they realised there was a charlatan in their midst? What was he doing two hundred and ninety-five years before his own time?

Wandering from room to room, they found no one. The whole house had changed, but he was relieved to find it uninhabited. She, however, found it quite disconcerting.

'They were here a moment ago,' she said, 'They are always playing their silly games and hiding from me.'

'Your parents?' he asked.

'No, silly, your aunt and uncle are in town. My brothers and sisters. They always leave me out. It makes me feel so ... unwanted.'

Edward's heart went out to her. He knew the pain of castigation more than most.

'Still, I'm here now,' he said, startled at his own admission. Elizabeth blushed.

The next few hours were spent in a timeless togetherness walking in the garden. The great oak trees he recognised from his garden he saw now as saplings just a few years old. Despite the unfamiliarity of his surroundings, his soul had never before felt such a sense of home. For the first time ever he could feel the warmth of the sun on his face, gaze upon the splendid colours that tenderly enfolded him, talk to someone who did not shy away from him. If it was a dream, he prayed that it would never end.

As the sun began to set, Elizabeth became increasingly agitated: her family were still mysteriously absent.

'I am beginning to worry about them,' she confided. 'We really ought to look again. You try that way, and I will go this.' Edward agreed; he would have done anything she asked. As he walked away his heart went with her, but he must do as she wished: pleasing her was all that mattered. He rounded the corner of one of the old rustic outbuildings when suddenly everything began to swirl and close in around him. His vision began to constrict until everything went black. He felt dizzy, his legs began to shake and buckle. Like a drunken man, he clutched the wall in desperation, but fell anyway, violently knocking his head.

When he awoke he shouted 'Elizabeth, Elizabeth!' The gloom told him that it might be night. He stood up and ran to the window ... window? Before he could check his actions, he had pulled apart the curtains and an agonising shaft of sunlight seared into his eyes. He snapped them shut and slumped half-blinded to the floor. Had all this isolation robbed him of his faculties of judgement? What had happened to him? His head pulsed and throbbed; whatever had happened had left a very real bruise. It must have been a flight of fancy ... how else would he have been able to understand the spoken word of Jacobean England so fluently when it would have been so markedly different in actuality? It must have been a dream.

The weeks passed and his solitary, lonely existence continued as before. Out of curiosity, he decided to trace the ownership of his parents' house. The only book he could find on local history in his own library seemed to suggest his ancestors had acquired the property sometime between 1610 and 1620. No records existed for the earlier period.

After a few months, all had been consigned to memory and its shallow grave, when one particularly lonely evening his sleep was once again disturbed. He roused himself from his hypnogogic state and into a full illuminated consciousness to find himself immersed in the decor of the early seventeenth century. Once again he recognised the unfamiliar familiarity. There was a gentle tap on the door.

'Come in,' he said rather gingerly. Delicately the divine features of his beloved Elizabeth appeared.

'Where did you go last night? I found the others, but then we couldn't find you any-where.'

'Oh, I ... I just came back here. I couldn't find you either and I didn't feel well.'

'Oh, I am sorry. Never mind,' she continued excitedly, 'They really are going away today, so we can have the day to ourselves. Would you like to go riding?'

That day spent with Elizabeth was the happiest day he had ever had. When they returned that night, he had quite forgotten his tenuous hold on reality and what or who he was. When he retired to bed, he clutched the sheets as hard as he could, in affirmation. They were very real indeed. Could they be the haven, the hold which he hoped for; what, if anything, would be? He was desperate. Here he wanted to stay, but already something was pulling him away.

The next morning, he awoke and instinctively knew. All his hopes and dreams fell on barren soil; this was no different. The dreary, drab room closed in like a coffin. Could there ever be any escape?

Slowly the visits to 1615 came with greater regularity, yet however long the passage of time in his own era in 1615 just a moment or two had passed. As the years in the twentieth century trundled towards the first great war, so his visits continued.

'Elizabeth,' he said one day, by now feeling sure enough of their bond of affection for such familiarity, 'would you tell me about your family?'

'Don't be so silly,' she said, 'they are your family as well!'

He had forgotten; she thought him her cousin. Rather flustered he continued, 'Could you tell me what happened during my trip abroad?'

'One day,' she whispered, 'one day.'

———————

The love of the two continued to grow with only the ardour a young heart can know. Though he knew they could never marry – not simply because they were cousins but because he was not a part of her time, nor she his – he also knew that the affection they both now nurtured was, at least for him, a partial deception. But could such passion be quashed? Conversely, the opposite seemed to be happening, until one day the two young paramours loved one another utterly.

The next few visits were awkward and strained. Still, he had not met any members of her family – indeed, any tie to family seemed cumbersome and difficult. To the two young lovers, any bond other than to each other disappeared. Her trust in him, he began to feel, was misplaced. What sort of person was he to elicit the force of love in someone so naive, when only he knew his dark and sickly secret?

Never could he fully reciprocate her love. He felt himself to be some stealthy incubus condemned to haunt and perpetrate hideous acts and cause untold misery.

'Please, Elizabeth, tell me what happened when I was abroad,' he insisted a few weeks after that fateful day.

'Please ... it is so painful,' she winced.

'Please – what happened to our family?'

'Our branch of the family,' she continued, with short gulped and laboured breaths, 'had to change its name, owing to the purge on Catholics. When we moved here, we changed our name from Gray to Wheatley to avoid the purge.'

'Gray to Wheatley,' he murmured, 'Gray to Wheatley! Elizabeth Gray! My God, you are one of my ancestors!'

'Stop it!' she cried, 'How can I be when you and I are of the same age?'

———

'Elizabeth Gray!' he wailed, 'Elizabeth Gray!'

'Stop it! Just stop it! It's not going to alter the fact that I am going to have your child ... '

Suddenly everything froze. Only then did the full horror of everything illuminate a perception previously clouded. He was the perpetrator of his own affliction! It had lain dormant through all those generations, only to execute justice on its original culprit. His father had been right all along: passion did equate with sin, did equate with guilt. If they had been allowed to live their natural lives in a natural way, she would never have had to change her name, and he would have known from the start that they were related. Her family would not have had to change their name to avoid persecution, his family would never have had an offspring to be ashamed of; whom they believed to be a punishment for a long-forgotten act. The chains of morality were chains of guilt. What had started out so right was now so wrong ... so very wrong.

In a Perfect World

The cool crystal pool looked very inviting as the crepuscular shadows gave way to the cool jewelled kisses of Diana, child of the sky. Latona was beckoning and covered everything like black mercury. Unerring arrows fell lovingly upon Endymion as he died an ephemeral death, only to arise Lazarus-like as the circle comes to its close.

Jade and emerald fell from the fresh and sparkling trees into the water. Eden-like, and unspoilt. All was silent, all was bliss. Untouched by the filthy hand of man, it breathed with a promise to change and alter and imperceptibly turn all that is bad to good.

Just as one can only know sweetness by contrasting it with sourness, so it is that true unity only comes when opposites are unified. No objectivity can come from either left or right, dark or shade, happiness or sadness. So it was with humanity. Yet everywhere the deformity of feminine grace and masculine virility persisted. In the majority of the protagonists the hideous façade was still paraded as the only way; indeed the dichotomy, the impassable gulf, was seen as a wonderful thing. A million years of evolution had brought us to this! The conquest, the battle of constantly displaying all one's wiles to their full advantage, was never to be seen as anything less than an epitome of a possible partner for the propagation of an effete and degenerate species. How wonderful if there could exist the *übermensch* that could combine the two – able to transcend any trial or tribulation relationships

———

bring! No jealousy, no preconceptions or ugliness, that often are the attributes so esteemed in any gender.

So it was that the small town had thrown up two such individuals, uncomfortable with their sex. She felt the narrow confines of her environment all too painfully. Closing in, they crushed out of her the joy to live. Local girls she had once called friends she now perceived as the worthless wretches they truly were. Only the local prostitutes she deemed to be honest. With an ironic eye, she watched her former friends parading in pairs, hoping to catch the eye of any available man. Such frivolous determination! One would think that their life depended upon It. Occasionally 'Prince Charming' did come along, but their own stupidity usually excluded love in preference to the jealous friend who always came first. Their small imagination left everything that really mattered closed and dormant to them. None had any aspiration to achieve anything more than a wealthy husband to ensure they would always be provided for. Why could they not cut the ties of their self-imposed bondage – reach out and clutch a world that lay in store like an autumn harvest. Instead they continued in their narrow little confines gossiping over social events they imbued with magnitude. How she hated them! How she hated herself for being the same sex as they! She felt tied to them by upbringing and environment. She hated the men who complied with them. They really did deserve each other. If only she were a man, then she might be accepted for herself, or escape to find herself and independence without having to use her sex to obtain a shallow reflection of it.

The other was a man. How he hated his sex! Too kind-hearted for an unkind world, he was an easy target for any hard man to prove his own virility upon; the physical beatings by such men still hurt. He lay all his fractured senses bare until the elements scorched them and washed them away, until the act of feeling became difficult, and he began to fear retribution for trying to do so. For him, love and beauty overrode alcohol and lust. His body he despised. The thinning hairline, the distended veins in his arms the coarse hair on his body, his large blunt features. How could he reconcile all this and then partake in the obscene parody which the courting ritual had become? How he longed to be a woman! To be allowed to be sensitive, to procreate, to give birth to a tiny child which could then be the sole receptacle for his love! But how could he escape? In a man's world he would always be a failure, an outcast. Not only was his physique lacking, his attitude was also sadly wrong: he lacked the self-righteousness, the aggression needed to be a 'real man'. There never would be a vocation for him. Nature had singled him out; it was a role he would have to play until the bitter end.

But the dissatisfaction did not stop there. In such a small town, the juxtaposition of sexes, and therefore the observation of their fraternisation, is hard to endure when one feels excluded, especially when the virtues lauded by others are anathema to oneself. It quickly escalates into an intense misanthropy. So it was with them both.

As the moon coolly beat on the pool, two great minds individually made one decision: suicide. The arcane and archaic woodland gently shimmered and swayed before them.

IN A PERFECT WORLD

Breezes that had seen the first man light the first fire would now witness a new birth. Destiny, previously thought so cruel, had seemingly changed her mind. Salvation was now within their grasp.

On opposite sides of the pool they stood, split by a liquid ebony. Both were naked as they penetrated the still waters. In they plunged: two bodies suspended in a matter that caressed every part of them. Water lapped against them both; only the waters of transfiguration separated them; waters that were penetrating every part. In ecstasy, death seemed near. In ecstasy, two bodies swam … two bodies … two bodies … one body.

A transformation had taken place. Like Hermaphroditus and Salmacis, the two were united in a single body. All that was beautiful existed within its sensual and graceful form. Broken chains of conformity and expectation floated free and drifted to the bottom of the pool. A perfect union stepped forth, liberated.

Society's constraints cast aside! Now the wasted years' others spend in pursuit of one another could blossom into a thing of beauty. Apparent opposites had made a whole! No guilt for sensitivity, no obligation to pursue aggression: a phoenix – an angel – rising anew in an epicene swirl. One body, one soul, one mind, one spirit, a synthesis of beauty, the quintessence of perfection. They had found one another: love had found a way.

Love rode into town on an ass, befitting, it would seem, a being worthy of veneration. What lay ahead? All knowledge had died. Only by a process of empiricism could a path be paved forward.

But the microcosm is subject to the macrocosm. The streets grew nearer and nearer. Human hostility began to coil and crouch and

———

prepare to attack; the ridiculous in fear of the sublime. The being before them was flawless. No solace was afforded. In the presence of a deity, the deity becomes a mirror reflecting every imperfection, ugliness, and oh so short life of those that gaze upon it. The truthfulness of beauty was all too much for them.

A line of people appeared on the streets, their faces twisted and contorted by their own failure. The town fell silent. Suddenly a rock was thrown, then another, then another. The rural byways offered a plentiful supply of ammunition, which was readily used. Soon love lay dead. There was cause for celebration. The ordinary revere the average, are hostile to the transcendent. But they continued to gaze at love. To them love was freakish. The appalling mediocrity of their gaze withered what was new and which now lay before them until, finally, all that was left was a pile of dry ashes.

The philistines congratulated themselves on their success as the new god died, ridiculed and ostracised.

Printed in Dunstable, United Kingdom

70892287R00084